WAZEM & AUBIN

SNOW DAY

Life Drawn

WILLIAMS & SON
Jesus
SAVES

PIERRE WAZEM
Writer

AUBIN
Artist

•

MARK BENCE
Translator

•

ALEX DONOGHUE, FABRICE SAPOLSKY
US Edition Editors

AMANDA LUCIDO
Assistant Editor

MAXIMILIEN CHAILLEUX
Original Edition Editor

JERRY FRISSEN
Senior Art Director

FABRICE GIGER
Publisher

Rights and Licensing - licensing@humanoids.com
Press and Social Media - pr@humanoids.com

SNOW DAY
This title is a publication of Humanoids, Inc. 8033 Sunset Blvd. #628, Los Angeles, CA 90046.

Library of Congress Control Number: 2018954820

Life Drawn is an imprint of Humanoids, Inc.

WILLIAMS & SON
JESUS SAVES

SCHOOL BUS

JOE'S MARKET
FOOD STORE
OPEN
FRUITS AND VEGETABLES

DINER
OPEN
DINER

LUNCH
Budweiser

JOHN F. KENNEDY
1917-63

POST

J SPENCER
SHERIFF

SHERIFF
F. BOSEMAN CO
SHERIFF FORT BOSEMAN DEPT.
CLANG

GODDAMMIT, SPENCER...
SHERIFF OFFICE
SLAM

...ARE YOU OUTTA YOUR MIND?

COFFEE?

I AIN'T HERE TO DRINK NO DAMN *COFFEE!* I CAME TO PICK UP *YOU-KNOW-WHO!*

GOD*DAMN*, WHAT'S GOTTEN INTO YOU?

YOU *KNOW* THAT I NEED THEM THREE!
TEXACO
THEY WENT A LITTLE TOO FAR THIS TIME, *ROSS*...

SURE YOU DON'T WANT SOME COFFEE?

ALRIGHT, ALRIGHT, MAYBE THEY WENT A *LIL'* TOO FAR...

...AND SO THEY GOT TO SPEND THE NIGHT LOCKED UP FOR IT... BUT *NOW* THEY GOTTA GO TO WORK, *GODDAMMIT!*

INSULTING AN OFFICER OF THE LAW, PLUS ASSAULT AND BATTE--
ARE YOU *YANKIN'* *MY CHAIN?*

YA KNOW WHERE YOU CAN STICK YOUR "INSULTS," *HUH?* NOW, LET THEM THREE FELLAS *OUTTA* YOUR DAMN SHACK AND CHANGE YOUR *GODDAMN* TUNE!

I'LL MAKE YOUR LIFE *HELL* IF YOU DON'T SEE REASON, ***YOU ASSHOLE!***
YOU *KNOW* WHO RUNS THIS TOWN, DON'T YOU?

GODDAMNIT, HAVE YOU *TOTALLY* LOST YOUR MIND?

HEY! WHAT THE *HELL'S* GOTTEN INTO YOU ALL OF A SUDDEN?
BOOM

THEY CROSSED THE LINE, ROSS.

AND IF YOU PLAN ON STAYING AWHILE, PLEASE SHUT THE DOOR. IT'S KINDA COLD OUTSIDE...
SHERIFF OFFICE

SHERIFF
OFFICE

SLAM

I'M GONNA GET THE MAYOR, YA HEAR!

HMM...

WELL, SHERIFF, GONNA HAVE TO LET US GO NOW, *HUH?!*

SHOULDA KEPT OUT OF IT, SPENCER!
YEAH, *SPENCER!* BETCHA SHITTIN' YER PANTS, NOW!

HA, HA, HA, HA!
MEOW...

PHILCO
MRRRU...

I DID RIGHT TO ARREST THEM, *EH?*
DIDN'T I, KITTY-CAT?

ANYWAY, THEY'RE STILL SO DRUNK THEY MIGHT JUST GO AND SLICE OFF A THUMB, OR A WHOLE HAND, AT THAT LOUSY FACTORY.

IT'S NOT THAT THEY'RE BAD GUYS. JUST A LITTLE ON THE *STUPID* SIDE...

RIFF
FICE

THIS *ASSHOLE* WON'T LET 'EM GO!

I SWEAR HE'S LOST HIS DAMN MIND!

THIS TRUE, SPENCER?

THEY CROSSED THE LINE, MR. MAYOR.
AHA.
YOU SEE!

SHERIFF FORT BOSEMAN DEPT
SHERIFF OFFICE
THIS GODDAMN WEATHER'S MESSIN' WITH HIS HEAD!

CALM DOWN, *CALM DOWN.* THE SHERIFF'S GOT RESPONSIBILITIES. HE HAS TO MAKE SURE THERE'S NO COMMOTION IN TOWN SO THAT DECENT FOLK CAN SLEEP EASY, YA KNOW.

THAT'S RIGHT, MR. MAYOR. MY POINT EXACTLY.

WELL, NOW THAT'S ALL SAID AND DONE, YOU CAN JUST LET OUR THREE ROWDIES GET OFF TO WORK. SEEMS LIKE THEY'VE BEEN PUNISHED ENOUGH.
SORRY, MR. MAYOR, BUT THOSE THREE ARE STAYING HERE.
OH MY GOD!
SHERIFF
BOSEMAN CO.
SHERIFF
FORT
SHERIFF
OFFICE

DON'T OVERDO IT, NOW, SPENCER. WHERE'S THE POINT IN THAT?

JUST CARRY ON NICELY, AS USUAL, AND DON'T OVERDO IT, YA HEAR?

DON'T MAKE ME MAD, NOW, SPENCER. YOU'RE A NICE FELLOW. BUT THIS IS GETTIN' *RIDICULOUS*. YOU'RE BLOWIN' IT OUT OF PROPORTION. THEY WERE ONLY BEIN' A LIL' ROWDY, PLUS TODAY'S A NEW DAY.
THERE'S MORE TO IT THAN THAT, MR. MAYOR. PLUS THEY MIGHT HURT THEMSELVES.

LISTEN, MR. ROSS NEEDS HIS MEN TO HELP RUN THE FACTORY. THEY GOT *PUNISHED*, AND NOW THEY HAVE TO *WORK*. WE CAN'T PARALYZE THE WHOLE FACTORY, NOW, CAN WE?
HE'S GOT PLENTY OF OTHERS...

...AND THOSE THREE DON'T JUST "WORK" AT THE FACTORY...

SHERIFF
SHERIFF FORT BOSEMAN DPT.

BAM

HE, HE, HE...
WALKED INTO A *DOOR* AGAIN, DID YA, SPENCER?

HELLUVA BAD HABIT...
HA, HA, HA...!

A DRAFT MUSTA BLOWN HIM INTO IT!
THE POOR LIL' THANG!

HEE, HEE...!
HA, HA, HA...!
WE OUGHTA STICK *LEAD* IN HIS LIL' BOOTIES!

HE HE HE
HA HA HA HA HA HA HA HA HA HA HA

HEE, HEE...
ALRIGHT, THAT'LL DO!
HA, HA, HA!
SHERIFF FORT BOSEM DEP
AWWW, BOO HOO...

BEST WATCH YOUR STEP GOIN' FORWARD, SPENCER. GETCHER *PRIORITIES* SORTED OUT...

...I DON'T WANNA HAVE TO WRITE TO THE *DISTRICT MARSHAL*.

AND YOU SHOULD GO CLEAR UP ROUTE 28. TOWN'LL BE CUT OFF BEFORE WE KNOW IT!

IT'LL HELP YOU THINK STRAIGHT!

HEY...

SPEED
LIMIT
55

SHERIFF

JOE'S
MARKET

LOW CLEARANCE
WEIGHT
LIMIT
3
TONS

JOE'S MARKET

EMMA?

EMMA?

JOE'S MARKET

COFFEE, SHERIFF?

I'D LOVE SOME.
JOE'S MARKET

I JUST HAD ONE, BUT IT DIDN'T GO DOWN TOO WELL...

GOD, WHAT HAPPENED TO YOUR FACE, SHERIFF?
THERE WAS A BRAWL LAST NIGHT...

...AND ONE MORE THIS MORNING.

SPENCER... WHAT ON EARTH ARE YOU DOING IN THIS TOWN?
MY JOB.

AND I PLAN ON DOING IT RIGHT.

I DID YOUR SHOPPING ON THE WAY... GOT YOU SOME BROWNIES.
JOE'S MARKET

YOU HAD A *VISITOR?*
IT WAS MY HUSBAND.
JOE'S MARKET

HE COMES BACK SOMETIMES.
?

I...
YES, YES, YES, HE'S *DEAD*, I KNOW, I KNOW.

NO NEED TO KEEP REMINDING ME **EVERY FIVE MINUTES, MR. SPENCER!**

YOU POOR THING, YOU'RE A REAL *BOY OF TODAY.*

YOU MODERN BOYS GET WORKED UP ABOUT *GHOSTS,* BUT EATING CRAP AND LIVING ON TOP OF A STINKY FACTORY BELCHING OUT POLLUTION DOESN'T BOTHER YOU.

HEE, HEE, HEE...

IT JUST ISN'T RIGHT!

IT'S A *HUGE* MISTAKE.

THIS IS NO TOWN FOR YOU, SPENCER.

JUST LOOK AT YOU. YOU'RE *HURTING* YOURSELF.

I DIDN'T DO IT TO *MYSELF*...
THIS IS NO PLACE FOR YOU. I'VE BEEN TELLING YOU FOR AGES!

LOOK AT THIS...

"...THAT'S MY FATHER."

IN 1890. SEE HOW STRONG HE WAS? YOU HAD TO BE STRONG TO SETTLE HERE. YOU HAD TO BE TOUGH. TOUGH AND TALL.

THAT'S THE TOWN.

JIM'S STORE
AUCTIONS
SAINT L
EMPORT

"YOU'RE NOTHING LIKE THEM, SPENCER."
JIM'S STO
AUCTION

SO DON'T EVEN TRY TO BE.

I HAVE A LOT TO DO TODAY, EMMA.

GOT SOME *OFFENDERS* TO ARREST...

MAKE SURE YOUR STOVE STAYS LIT, AND GIVE MY REGARDS TO YOUR HUSBAND.

STOCK HOUSE
FOUN
DEPART

BECKY?

WHATCHA DOING OUT HERE?
JUST LOOKIN'.

LOOKING AT *WHAT?* THERE'S NOTHING HERE.
I WAS LOOKIN' AT THE FACTORY. IT'S *BEAUTIFUL!*

BEAUTIFUL?!
YEAH, IT *TURNS* ME ON!

CLIMB IN! I'LL TAKE YOU BACK TO TOWN. YOU'LL *FREEZE TO DEATH* OUT HERE.

YA LOVE YOUR BIG SNOWPLOW, DON'T YOU NOW?

YOU LOOK SO *TINY* IN IT! *HEE HEE.*

FEELS SO GOOD WITH YOU...

AT LEAST *YOU* UNDERSTAND ME!

NO.

NO *WHAT?*
NO, I ACTUALLY DON'T GET YOUR THEATRICS AT ALL!

WHY'S THERE NO MOVIE THEATER IN *FORT BOSEMAN?*

WE AIN'T EVEN GOT A DAMN LIBRARY!
AS FAR AS I KNOW, ANIMALS CAN'T READ...

I'M GONNA BE AN *ACTRESS!*
YEAH, YEAH...RIGHT.

YOU'RE NO FUN.

IF I DO SOMETHIN' STUPID, WILL YOU PUT ME IN JAIL?

HOW DID YOU GET ALL THE WAY OUT HERE, ANYWAY?
THROUGH THE WOODS.

AREN'T YOU AFRAID TO GO THROUGH THE WOODS?
NOPE! I AIN'T SCARED A' *NOTHIN'!*

MATTER OF TIME...

I'D STILL LIKE YOU TO PUT ME IN JAIL, JUST TO SEE HOW IT IS!

WITHOUT FOOD OR WATER. YOU COULD BEAT ME UP SOMETIMES...
CLICK

BUT NOT *TOO* MUCH...

YOU COULD EVEN **PLAY** WITH ME...

JUST A LITTLE, FOR **FUN**...!

INN
LUNCH
OPEN

Budweiser

SHERIFF?

YOU BEEN FIGHTING?
YOU KNOW THAT'S NOT REALLY MY STYLE.

THIS TOWN AIN'T SO BIG, IS IT?

YOU MUST KNOW WHAT MAKES IT TICK.

DID WE BREAK UP BECAUSE I WASN'T STRONG – OR *TALL* – ENOUGH?

KATHLEEN?

WHAT ARE YOU *DOING* HERE, SPENCER? IN THIS TOWN, I MEAN...
NOT REALLY MY KIND OF PLACE, *HUH?*

WHY D'YOU THINK THEY APPOINTED *YOU*, SPENCER?

ALL THAT'S GONNA CHANGE.

I LEFT YOU BECAUSE IT *NEVER* CHANGES. *THAT'S* WHY.

THERE'S ALWAYS SOME MORON TO MAKE YOU BELIEVE IN...IN...*BULLSHIT!*

AND THINGS ONLY GET HARDER AFTERWARDS! ...WHAT'LL YOU HAVE TO EAT?
AFTER WHAT?

AHHH, SHIT! WHAT'LL IT BE, SPENCER?
DON'T YOU LIKE SHORT GUYS?

DON'T BE AN ASS! WHAT'LL IT BE?
DYNAMITE COMES IN SMALL PACKAGES...

WHAT'LL IT BE?!
THE *USUAL*. WHY BOTHER ASKING?

Old Fash
SNIDER
OLD FASHI
CHILI SA

LUNCH

DINER
LUNCH

THE FORT BOZEMAN INN
DINER
LUNCH

THE FORT BOZEMAN INN
DINER
LUNCH

I AM THE WAY, THE TRUTH, AND THE LIFE...
INER

THE FORT BOZEMAN INN
DINER
LUNCH

Old Fash
SNIDE
OLD FASH

WHAT *HAPPENED* LAST NIGHT?
?

AND WHY AREN'T YOU TWO AT WORK?

WAS IT *YOU* HE WAS FIGHTING?

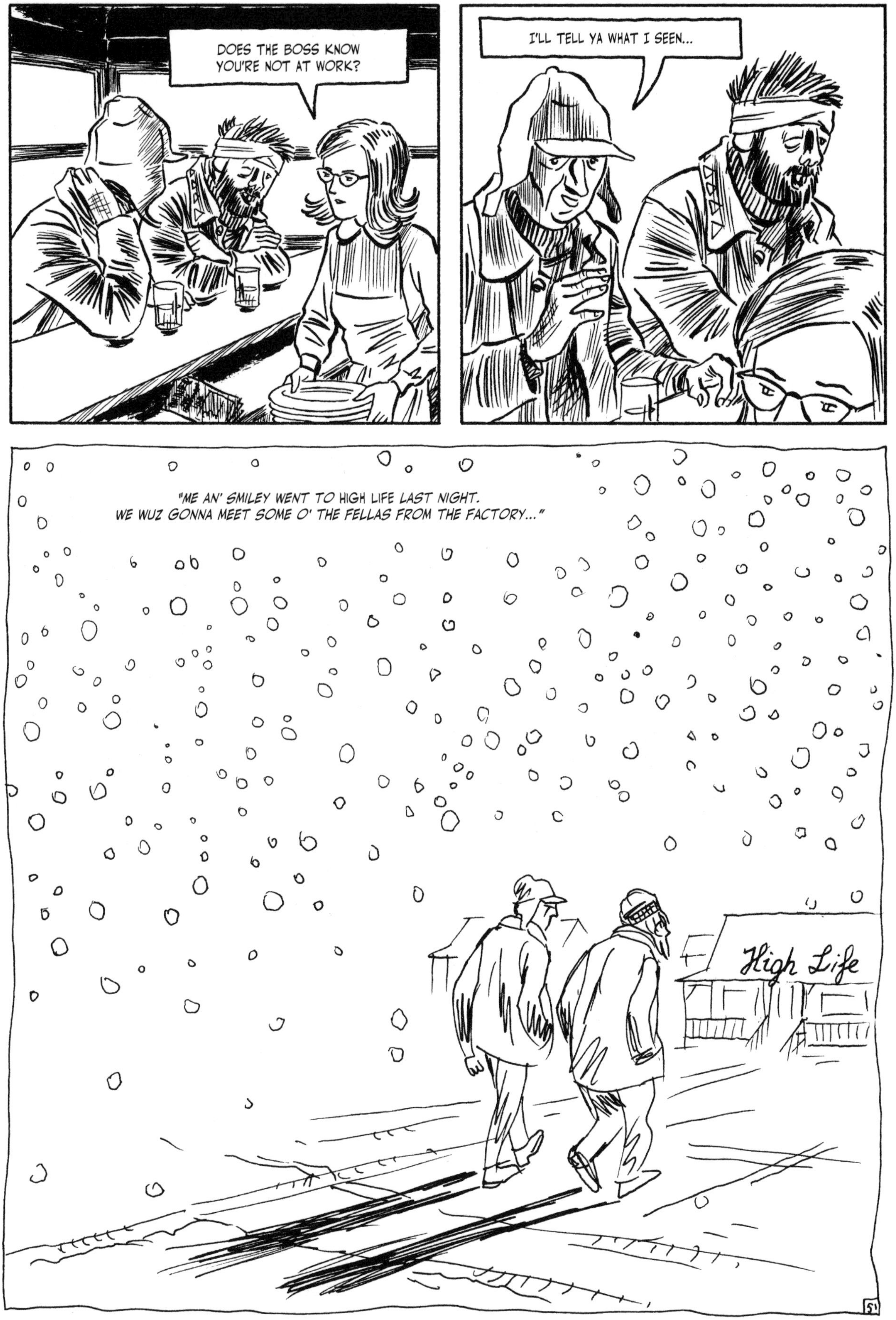

"ME AN' SMILEY WENT TO HIGH LIFE LAST NIGHT.
WE WUZ GONNA MEET SOME O' THE FELLAS FROM THE FACTORY..."

High Life

"SPENCER WUZ PARKED UP IN HIS CAR JUST NEARBY. 'EV'NIN' SHERIFF,' I SAYS."

"WE WUZN'T THE FIRST THERE, NOR THE LAST NEITHER. THERE WUZ KULIC, O'LEARY, THOMPSON, FALCONETTI... WUZ ONLY US FACTORY GUYS, YA KNOW."
High Life

"YOUDA THOUGHT IT WUZ UNION CLUB NIGHT, THE WAY THEY WUZ YELLIN'..."
ENOUGH!
BEER

WE'RE ALL *SCREWED!*

THE CONDITIONS ARE GODDAMN *TERRIBLE!*

RIGHT!

YEAH!

COLLINS LOST HIS *HAND!*

SO DID MACPHERSON LAST MONTH!

"ME AN' SMILEY JUST LET 'EM TALK!"

"A BIT LATER, I GO OUT TO PISS A HOLE IN THE SNOW. I'D BIN WANTIN' TA TAKE A LEAK SINCE I GOT THERE..."

"I COULD HEAR THE OTHERS YELLIN' INSIDE."

"SAME AS ALWAYS..."

"THE BOSSMAN
AND HIS HEAVIES."

"I WUZ DONE PISSIN' JUST AS SPENCER WUZ STEPPIN' OUT TO SMOKE."

"BEER GETS ME PISSIN',
I TELL YA!"

"THE BOSS'S HEAVIES
AIN'T TOO KEEN ON THE KINDA
TALK I MENTIONED EARLIA..."
"I WALKED IN AFTER
SPENCER. AIN'T TOO SURE
WHAT HE EXPECTED..."

"I WENT TO FIND SMILEY. HE'D'VE DONE BETTER TO GO TAKE A LEAK, LIKE I DID..."

"THEN ALL OF SUDDEN, SPENCER STEPS UP AND SAYS:"
ENOUGH! YOU THREE ARE COMING WITH ME.

?
?
?

YOU'RE UNDER ARREST.
YA FEELIN' OKAY, SHERIFF?

"FOR DISTURBING THE PEACE, ASSAULT, AND BEING DRUNK IN PUBLIC,' HE ADDS!"
I'LL BE DAMNED!

"I PICKED SMILEY UP AND WE LEFT IN A HURRY."

"SPENCER, HE LEFT IN A HURRY TOO..."

DIDN'T YOU HEAR ME?
YOU'RE UNDER ARREST!

YOU STARTED THIS BRAWL, SO NOW YOU'RE UNDER ARREST!

HOLD OUT YOUR HANDS...
JESUS CHRIST! YA WANT SOME MORE, *THAT IT?*
STOP...

"IT WUZ LIKE HE HADN'T HAD ENOUGH!"

"CUZ SPENCER JUST SAID IT AGAIN:"

I WON'T REPEAT IT. YOU'RE COMING WITH ME!

"COULDN'T BELIEVE THE BOSS'S HEAVIES EVEN LET HIM TALK TO 'EM THAT WAY!"

"DUNNO WHY, BUT THEY FOLLOWED THE SHERIFF. MAYBE THEY DIDN'T KNOW THEMSELVES. P'RAPS THEY WUZ TOO WASTED TO KNOW."

"THEN SPENCER COMES OUT WITH:"
YOU CAN'T DEAL WITH THE COLD BY BREAKING THE THERMOMETER.
"WHATEVER THAT MEANT..."

ANYWAYS... I'D NEVER HAVE BELIEVED IT...NOT WIT' THAT KINDA SHERIFF, YA KNOW?
SHERIFF

DINER
Well.
~~I still love you~~
and my love
isn't small
at all!

SHERIFF

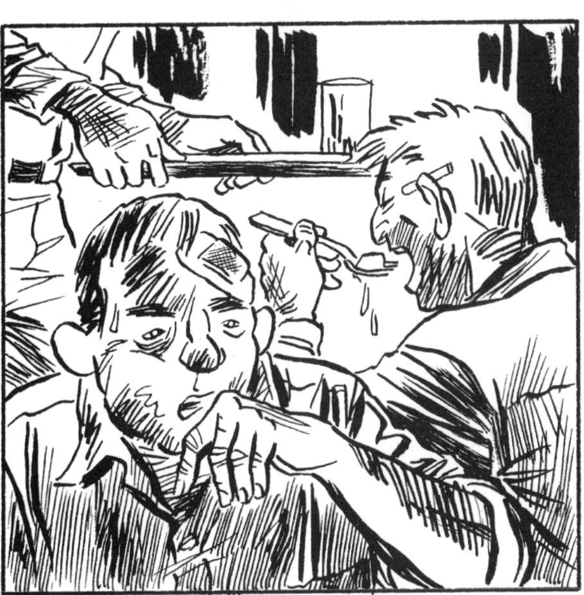

CLICK

SHHH...

?

AND THE THIRD?

THE *THIRD*?

YA DON'T WANNA DO THIS, SHERIFF.

IT'S NOTHING PERSONAL. YOU'RE JUST A LITTLE STUPID. THAT'S NOT YOUR FAULT.

BUT IF YOU DON'T WANT TO MAKE THINGS WORSE, YOU'D BETTER SHUT UP.

THE THIRD, I SAID.
HE'S STILL IN THE FACTORY, SHERIFF. DOWN IN THE PUMP ROOM.

NOBODY LEAVES THIS PLACE UNTIL I GET BACK.

THE REST OF YA CAN FINISH YOUR LUNCH.

WHAT'S HIS NAME?
BIG BEAR.

THAT FIGURES.

PUMP
ROOM

!
CLONG
CLONG

MEOW.

CLANG!

HA! HA! HA!
YA CAME ALL THIS WAY,
SHERIFF!

RIGHT DOWN
INTO MY LAIR!

I GOT SLIGHTLY
INTERRUPTED THIS
MORNING...

...AND I HATE
TO LEAVE A JOB
UNFINISHED.

YOU'RE ONE HELLUVA
LEECH, SHERIFF!

GODDAMMIT, WHAT WUZ IT MADE YA LOSE YER MIND LIKE THAT LAST NIGHT?

YA USED TO BE *HARMLESS*, SHERIFF. NEVER PISSED NOBODY OFF!

YOU NEVER KNOW WHEN IT'S ENOUGH. YOU ONLY KNOW WHEN IT'S *MORE* THAN ENOUGH.
WHAT'S THAT YOU'RE SAYIN'?

DROP THAT AND COME WITH ME.

BONG

YOU EVER GO HUNTING, BIG BEAR?
HUH?

SOMETIMES.

WHEN I GO HUNTING, I MAKE SURE I KILL THE ANIMAL WITH MY FIRST SHOT, SO IT DOESN'T *SUFFER.*

BECAUSE I HAVE SOME *RESPECT* FOR IT, YOU SEE.

CLICK!

GET IN THE BACK.

YOU CALLED HIM, DIDN'T YOU?

HE'S ON HIS WAY.
AND HE'S... HE'S *REAL* MAD.

I BET HE IS...

BRROOM

CRASH

DINER
LUNCH

SSCHHHHH

KLONG!

CREAK

I'M ARRESTING YOU, ROSS, FOR OBSTRUCTING AN OFFICER ON DUTY...

...MALTREATING YOUR EMPLOYEES, AND LOTS OF OTHER ISSUES THAT NEED LOOKING INTO.

YOU... YOU'VE...LOST YOUR *DAMN* MIND, SPENCER!

I'M... I'M GONNA HAVE TO REPORT THIS TO THE MARSHAL.
GET UP, ROSS.

WHAT THE HELL'S GOIN' ON HERE?!

YOU'RE JUST IN TIME. I'M GOING TO HAVE TO ARREST YOU, TOO, MR. MAYOR.
?

DAMN IT ALL, SPENCER! WHAT'S THE *MATTER* WITH YOU?

IT WAS *ME* WHO APPOINTED YOU, FOR *GOD'S SAKE!*

YOU FORGETTIN' THAT?
HE'S GONE CRAZY!

TO ACKNOWLEDGE WE ARE NAKED OF *ALL* VIRTUE, SO WE MAY BE *CLOTHED* BY GOD...
ARE YOU READY FOR THE RAPTURE

READY FO
THE RAPTU
EMPTY OF ALL GOOD, SO WE MAY BE FILLED BY HIM...

GET LOST, BUTCH!
LAME, SO WE MAY BE GUIDED BY THE LORD.

CONFIDE IN OUR LORD JESUS...
I SAID GET LOST!

!

ARE YOU READY FOR THE RAPTURE
JESUS IS THE WAY, THE TRUTH...
OH CHRIST! SPENCER...

BAM

AH, AAAH, AAAAH...
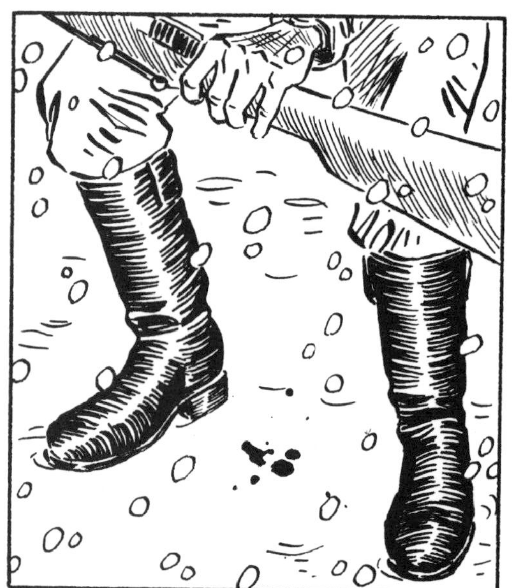

THE WAY, THE TRUTH, AND THE LIFE. ALL THE BELIEVERS...
ARE YOU READY FOR THE RAPTURE

BASTARD!

IT WAS AN ACCIDENT, RIGHT? *THE BASTARD!*

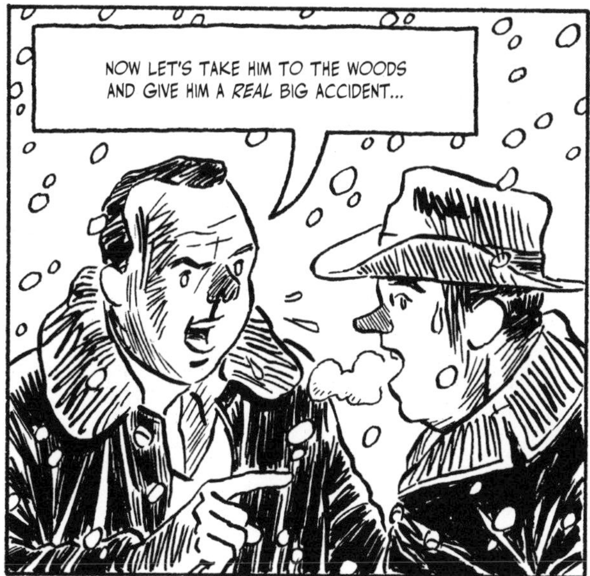
NOW LET'S TAKE HIM TO THE WOODS AND GIVE HIM A *REAL* BIG ACCIDENT...

C'MON! GET UP, YOU BASTARD!
HEY! UNCUFF US, DAMMIT!

ENOUGH!
Dynamite
N. 003C6

?

ENOUGH!
CARVER INC

YEAH! WE'RE GONNA BLOW YOU UP, YOU ASSHOLES!

DYNAMITE COMES IN SMALL PACKAGES, RIGHT?!

GO AHEAD. LET'S GET IT OVER WITH.
YOU WOULDN'T DARE, YOU *BITCH!* CHICKS AIN'T GOT NO BALLS...

PSHHHHH

YEAH... *BOOM!* **KABOOM!**

AAAARGH...

JESUS CHRIST!

?
HANDCUFF HIM. THEY'RE IN THE SNOWPLOW.
YOU OKAY, SPENCER?
JUST MY BELLY FAT...
FAT?! THERE AIN'T NONE ON YA!

GET IN.
IT'S OVER.

GET IN.
I'M FINE. IT'S JUST
A SCRATCH.

YOU CAN'T
SHOOT FOR
SHIT.

NOW DON'T DO ANYTHING DUMBER
THAN YOU ALREADY HAVE.

IT'D BE TOO MUCH FOR
SUCH A SMALL TOWN.

THE JUDGE'LL BE ALONG TOMORROW MORNING. YOU CAN CALL YOUR LAWYER IN THE MEANTIME.

TILL THEN, YOU HAVE THE RIGHT TO REMAIN SILENT, *ETC*...

KNOW WHAT, MR. MAYOR? YOU CAN'T DEAL WITH THE COLD BY BREAKING THE THERMOMETER...
?

WHAT'D YA SAY?
OH, NOTHING.

FORGET IT.

I MEANT THAT THE COLD'S *ALWAYS* THERE. THEN ONE DAY, IT JUST GETS *TOO* COLD.

THE LAST STRAW...
JUST DROP IT, ALRIGHT? I DON'T GET WHAT YOU'RE SAYIN' ONE BIT!

THAT'S BECAUSE YOU'RE A LITTLE STUPID, MR. MAYOR.

ALL THIS JUST 'CUZ THEY WERE LIL' *ROWDY?!*
THERE'S MORE TO IT THAN THAT, MR. MAYOR...

Dynamite

Dynamite

519 WILKINSO

?

DINER
Well,
I still love you
and my love
isn't small
at all!
I JUST
LOVE YOU.
SIMPLE AS
THAT!

I AGREE TO ANOTHER
"SHORT" TRIAL PERIOD!
DINER
Well, I still love you and my love isn't small at all!
I JUST LOVE YOU. SIMPLE AS THAT!

END.